WILD SURMISE
DOROTHY PORTER

lovely to meet you Bill

Dx

PICADOR
Pan Macmillan Australia

30/7/03

The characters and events in this book are fictitious and any
resemblance to real persons, living or dead, is purely coincidental.

First published 2002 in Picador by Pan Macmillan Australia
Pty Limited
St Martins Tower, 31 Market Street, Sydney

Copyright © Dorothy Porter 2002

All rights reserved. No part of this book may be reproduced
or transmitted in any form or by any means, electronic or mechanical,
including photocopying, recording or by any
information storage and retrieval system, without prior
permission in writing from the publisher.

National Library of Australia
Cataloguing-in-Publication data:

Porter, Dorothy Featherstone, 1954– .
Wild surmise.

ISBN 0 330 36380 8.

1. Emotions – Poetry. 2. Death – Poetry. I. Title.

A821.3.

Typeset in 11/17 Palatino by Midland Typesetters,
Maryborough, Victoria
Printed in Australia by McPherson's Printing Group

For Andy

Then felt I like some watcher of the skies
  When a new planet swims into his ken;
Or like stout Cortez when with eagle eyes
  He stared at the Pacific—and all his men
Look'd at each other with a wild surmise —

ON FIRST LOOKING INTO CHAPMAN'S HOMER
    John Keats

Behold now, standing before you, the man who
has pierced the air and penetrated the sky,
wended his way amongst the stars and
overpassed the margins of the world

LA CENA DE LE CENERI
    Giordano Bruno (1548–1600)

OCEANS

Europa

Let us travel
the three hundred and ninety million miles
to Jupiter's smoothest moon,
Europa.

You can't miss Jupiter,
hanging over its moon
in a whirling rainbow mass
of push, pull and poison.

Feel Europa's freezing
toxic silence.

You're standing on a raft
of thick alien ice,
but you're moving—
floating like a berg
on the deepest ocean
in the unknown world.

This is the roof, the shield
of a black liquid world,
where you may one day
drop like a warm stone.

A new world
where you might learn
colder lessons
than nothing.

As she knows it

The hooks and dreams and siren's songs
from the Galileo and Cassini probes
swarm luminescent
like deep water squid
on Alex Leefson's computer screen.

Life
as she doesn't know it
calls and calls
like a parching hunt.

Life
as she does know it
is the chat-show circuit
where Alex flamboyantly plays
astronomy's glamour girl
talking up
the Solar System's alien life
hidey holes
with a rapturous intimacy.

Astrobiology

Was this a kamikaze career move?

Taking up astrobiology's
butterfly net
and swatting at teases, guesses
and fairy dust?

In planetary science
I made exciting
but solid ground.

No one knew
no one talked
about celestial volcanoes
with more power
more public panache
than me.

I drew down
for packed halls
the slumbering gigantic cones
on pink Mars.

I conjured the Goddess of Love
stalking
with ancient pancake lava
footprints
across the lead-boiling lethal
surface of Venus.

I played sexy movies
of Io, Jupiter's live-wire moon,
erupting
with jagged spurts
of fiery green sulfur.

So when
did this latest infatuation
get a grip?

Why am I,
a happily childless woman,
now waiting
for Life
like a junkie waits
for a fix?

Perhaps I'm craving
that almighty hit
when I know
when I prove
Life.
Gloriously elsewhere.
Life.
Brazenly everywhere.

Bombs away

Alex was hopeless
at sitting by the phone.

When would Europa ring?

She would be perfectly happy
with a terse e-mail

    I'm alive

She remembers being cornered
by an aggressively acned Yankee
boy wonder engineer
at an exobiology conference
under a glacial air-conditioning vent
in the Houston Hilton,
his hands trembling
as he cradled an imaginary bomb

'What are we waiting for?
Just drop this little mother
on the ice
boom!
and watch my Ice Clipper
sail through the splash
and snatch those bugs
like flypaper.'

There were days when Alex
would have bombed Europa
to slush and stinking fish

just so she too
would know.

Always Mars

Where there's water
there's a chance,
a sniff,
a hope of life.

Was there still
somewhere,
lurking and seeping,
water on Mars?

Alex couldn't care.

It was always Mars.
Like a pink-skinned first son,
who got all the feverish
breath-holding celebratory
attention.

Always Mars.
As if Europa were a remote
and selfish daughter
who lived too far away
to be useful.

But perhaps Europa
was lucky,
like many an overlooked woman
she could settle intimately
and unmolested
into her secrets.

Water

My garden is no alien.

Greeting me
when it rains
with a goose-pimpling eucalyptus
embrace.

Our lemon tree glows
like a quenched prayer.

May it listen to mine.

Oh, Europa, please trust
and take me in.

Let me be the divining rod
    quivering
over your deep treasure
    of water.

Clear delirium

Bruno, forgive me,
for thinking about you
at a barbecue.

I've always loved you
just as much,
for having the icy guts
to knock back a crucifix
shoved at your hands
through the holy flames,
as for your clear delirium
of other worlds—

blasphemously countless
planets. moons. stars.
all brazen with life,
   a celestial standing ovation
      to your reckless gall.

In your time
they would have burnt me too,

for a venomous assortment
of mainly misogynist reasons.

But let me send you greetings,
and a waft of burnt sausage,
from these early years
of the twenty-first century.

Bruno, your bright cinders
are still blowing cruelly
into the dank eyes
of the orthodox.

Bless me
as your bold new breeze.

Help me make them
blink.

Europa's shadow

Jupiter shimmers
from Alex's computer screen.

Alex's ageing, bright eyes
lap over
her giant planet
aglow
with the whirling glitter
of ammonia clouds.

But Alex's loving
and probing gaze
snags
on the melanoma spot
of Europa.

Just its tiny shadow,
the moon itself
a little white pill
on the right of the screen.

An hallucinogen,
if recklessly swallowed,

lodging itself
like a stalking octopus
under the rocks
of the swallower's dreams.

Suddenly Alex calls out
to her husband, Daniel,
morosely muttering
over his marking.

She is his Europa,
and he shoves his students'
stilted stories
and pretentious poems
onto the floor.

What is it this time?

What dazzling snatch
of incomprehensible wonder
will she deign, briefly,
to share with him?

Daniel's epigram

My wife is no one's moon.
I am no one's sun.

Blue light

The morning begins bluely
for Daniel Morgan
with the light struggling
but glimmering
behind the winter drama
of stark bare trees

he's reading Ovid
in translation
but stops now and then
to watch the light
changing,
from a thick grey pink
to an airy thin blue
that he can feel expanding
in his lungs
like a gust of imagery.

He puts Ovid to one side,
praying to Ovid's gods, his gods,
to keep him this alert
this happily ravished by poetry
forever.

Melbourne coffee shops

Alex is a Sydney girl.
That shallow restlessness
always whingeing for water.

While I have measured out my life
in the morning newspaper
and espresso pleasure
of coffee shops.

Let Alex hunger for her Harbour.
Give me Brunswick Street,
and the warm view from Mario's
on a wild winter's day
when the street is flooding
with feral human traffic
elated with wind and walking
against the cold driving wet.

Coffee Dante

There's nothing like
a perfect coffee.

There's nothing like
that first sip
of a new Dante translation.

Does it have the right terza rima
aroma?

O, yes.
And once again
I'm swaying on the deck
of the best poetry
in the world.

Coffee Dante,
get me through this day.
Slip me
    your steam, your sweet froth.

Different ponds

Daniel smirks
as he puts down
a steaming pot of tea
for his wife

'How much is that doggy
in the window?'
he points at her bizarre
screen saver
blowing bubbles across the screen

'Priceless.'
Alex yawns
splaying her fingers in the air
like starfish
'It's my ichthyosaur.
He's extinct,
but watch for his pal.'

and a dolphin
almost boring
in its New Age cuteness
waggles into view

'Cousins?'
Daniel asks

Alex picks up
her fossil fish,
etched like an X Ray
on a jagged piece of clayey
slate,
and weighs it lovingly
in her hand

'Convergent evolution, darling,
where flippers
in one animal
are still flippers
in another completely different animal.'

she squeezes the fossil
and holds it to her ear
like a seashell

'If there is life
in the Europan sea,
if there is just enough

for them to fucking eat,
convergent evolution says
the critters of Europa
could look something
like our fish, our squid
our whales, our jellyfish.'

Daniel thinks suddenly
of Ovid's surreal
bestiality

'I can't see even randy old Jupiter'
he says pointing
at the ichthyosaur
'jumping that bugger.'

Alex nods blankly
and returns to the screen

and once again
they're paddling
in different ponds.

Teaching

Daniel used to enjoy teaching.
Three thousand years ago.

The usual whinge
about corporate dickheads
destroying Higher Education
was even tireder
than he was.

Some of his fellow lecturers
murmured amongst themselves
that all their Asian students
looked the same.

Daniel didn't discriminate.
All his students looked
and sounded
the same.
Fucking dull.

While Alex's ravenous brain
was launching itself

in a shower of psychic sparks
at Europa,
towards what reeking
stale-cabbage-soup
nursing home
was his cantankerous mind
shuffling?

The fertile egg

Alex sips on her Diet Coke,
feeling it burn down her throat
like an acidic amphetamine,
burping over the latest Europa
pics
she absent-mindedly wipes
her mouth
while her brain revs
and begins its white-hot
focus.

On some mornings
her mind
could ignite paper

what if   what if
her imagination stammers
staring at Europa's
cracked-eggshell surface

what if
the ice is protecting

the ocean
like a shell protects
the gummed-eyed chick?

What if
the ice were shielding
a marine sanctuary?
Not just a sprinkle
of struggling microbes?

It was always easier
to grow and live
big
in water.

What if
the ice were nurturing
a weightless world
of gliding blind giants?

Shocking

And when I first stick my hand
in Europa's water
will a shock pass
straight through me?

Like Michelangelo's Adam stretching
his finger to God's
will a shock pass
straight through me?

What will gush forth
when my rib is struck?

What unforetold creature will swim
through the umbilical cord
of this Eve's brain?

Anomalocaris

I'm drifting away
from the restaurant noise
and Daniel's amusing whingeing
about his boss—

the grilled prawn's head
leaks warm juice
through my fingers—

and my head floods
with Cambrian shallow water,
when the land was verboten
and Earth's warm sea teemed—

swimming a rippling swathe
through the sponges
is *anomalocaris*—

a robotic predator
with a struggling trilobite
in its shrimpish claws—

anomalocaris's digestive juices
go crazy
while I'm tasting
the salty wet light.

No briny nursery like this
likely
in the Europan ice black sea.

What abyss-flavoured thing
with starving electro-sensors
will home in
on my blind thrashings
    and bite off
        my calcium-rich head?

Niches

Alex lies dreamily
in the warm niche
of Daniel's arms

and thinks,
with a guilty smirk,
that it's easier to doze
in a warm niche
without the bombardment
of lust's charged particles

but
    and Alex shifts position
    as Europa seeps in
maybe niches would be
nothing
but sterile puddles of warm slush
without the energy-driving
smack
of radiation

the crackling hiss
of hit and miss

passion and poison

is Life's Law
the same for organic particles
as for human hearts?

accelerate me hard

and suddenly all the bacteria
in all Europa's, all Alex's,
warm niches
wave their flagella
in one wild accord.

The Venusian Sea

Water
  I prickle awake at four a.m.
    in the desert dark
      dreaming of water

O for a solo passage
  across the impossible
    Venusian Sea!

Water
  a wet green whiff—
the rusty Martian flood plains
  squawking into life

water
    my own bloodstream
      trilling with minerals
        whelped in the stars.

O for the El Dorado gold
  at the glimmering bottom
    of the taken-off-course
      white rapids spin!

Water, deep water,
   the dream in my side
      through which I'm dribbling.

Colour

This morning,
in Sydney
for the Extrasolar Planets Conference,
Alex's optic nerve pumps
a gush of colour
straight to her heart

there is a flash green lorikeet
hanging upside down
trembling an orange-red flower
on the thorny-barked coral tree

she can't hear or smell
a thing

it's all colour!
the light
surging into her eyes
while her heart trips
and blinks.

Could any other world
bring her eye's pulse
to this sublime boil?

Could her passion for colour
keep her earthed, keep her wilfully
in the dark?

Her photo

It's Phoebe.
Headlining the programme.
The celebrity Nay-Sayer.

It's Phoebe.
Nine years older.
Full colour spread
of the Universe whirling about her
like huge sparkling skirts.

Phoebe.
With a shorn pretty head
like an Emperor's clever
bemused catamite.

Phoebe staring down infinity
with her light green eyes
like a whiphand flicker
of chlorophyll.

Phoebe's cool hard proofs
of the accelerating universe
are making her famous

trust Phoebe to discover
the Universe is running away from us

who else would so revel
in a cosmic future of freezing
nothingness?

But that full know-it-all mouth
    the battle tilt of her chin
        those steady-state lovely cold eyes.

It's Phoebe.
Her image thriving and multiplying
in Alex's capitulating cells.

Even though it's light years
too late,
Alex tears out the page
  rips the Universe in half
    and scrunches Phoebe's photo
       into a tight hot accelerating ball.

At nine thousand feet

Alex first met Phoebe
at nine thousand feet

it was 1994

Alex had been married
to Daniel
for two quick hectic
happy years

later
Alex would say
at nine thousand feet
no one has any judgment

but deep in her own sea-level
heart
she would never let it go

some insistent part of her
would guzzle the dizzying oxygen
at nine thousand feet
with a phantom Phoebe forever

she accepted
between avid kisses
Phoebe's rules

this was a typical
Mauna Kea romance
'the real altitude sickness'
Phoebe had said
her arms wrapped around Alex
like a space blanket,
while blazing galaxies smoked
outside their window

'but'
and Alex would never forget
the dark turn in Phoebe's close
breathing
'I've got a life, a life
I never dreamed I'd have,
a life
of such mental freedom
no woman scientist alive
would risk,
risk for anything

no matter how lovely
no matter how tempting'

and so for the next supernova
month
Alex feasted in the present tense
and lived Hawaii with Phoebe
to the blood, bone and marrow.

Mauna Kea

Her brain shouldn't be doing
this

after the obligatory
twenty-four hours
at nine thousand feet
it shouldn't be
at fourteen thousand feet
this giddy

like looking at a whirring galaxy
in the lurid-lolly colours of infra-red
with a hangover

perhaps she hadn't anticipated
this racy religious awe
hung upside down
drooling nauseously
in her aching head.

But no suck
on an oxygen bottle

could calm
the giddying magnificence
of these observatory domes
bedded in lava litter
growing like glinting bulbs
from the peak
of this frozen volcano

no munch of chocolate
fumbled with blue numb
hands,
could ease
the squeeze on her lungs
   or make her heart's whirligig
        stop.

Ode to Keck

Alex couldn't wait to share
with Phoebe
her oxygen-starved first night
at fourteen thousand feet
on the glorious Keck telescope.

Reading the eruptions
on Jupiter's pustular moon, Io,
she'd felt so searingly close
her eyes stung
in the wheezing steam
of Io's acrid sulfur flares.

Hugging her coffee cup
at nine thousand feet
Alex didn't care
that her piddly lunar volcanoes
were no match
for Phoebe's ultra-butch project,
an infra-red zoom
to the black-hole core
of the Milky Way.

In the thawing bliss
of her new lover's face
Alex didn't care
she would never be a match
for Phoebe
in anything at all.

Married

Hawaii
never made Alex forget
she was married

she still grinned
on the phone to Daniel
relishing the salty savagery
of his jokes

a style of humour
bewildering to Phoebe's
good-natured Yankee
self-content.

Alex floated in the fantasy,
as lulling as the gorgeous
Pacific,
that she had everything—

a terrific marriage
with a funny devoted clever
man

plus
for the finite time being
(and god she was going to enjoy it)
an intoxication
a Bali Ha'i secret island
with a brilliant foreign lesbian
so sexy, so independent,
whom she'd never see again.

There were cakes
you could eat and have,
there were reefs
where the sharks came in
to be fed and tickled.

The Hawaiian octopus

Alex watches Phoebe's strong legs
flashing ahead of her
in the warm aqua reef off Kaua'i

and luxuriates
in the amniotic fluid
of sea. lover. wonder.

Watching Phoebe's white-fleshed
splash
she could be a reef shark
harmless but oh so watchfully
hungry

until she senses something
eyeing her
and her masked face turns
into the gaze
of a large octopus.

Its eerie
awareness.

not like the dopey butterfly fish
dangling around her
like a marine-themed mobile.

Amazing.
but all over
in a lightning second
dense with two sparking
nervous systems

the octopus vanishing
as if its brain waved a wand
fizzling
this tentacled lump
into the rock of the reef.

But Alex can hear
through the lull of the water
in her own brain's
deep stem
an unmistakable octopus
growl

now
under her floating flippers

a bit of reef,
old coral, patchy white weed,
is octopus.

Suddenly the rock breathes.

But when their optic nerves lock
again
the octopus jets off
                  backwards.

Bali Ha'i

Phoebe's fingers wake Alex up
the next morning

the mountain and the sea
out their five-star resort window
enchanted in a blue haze

but something is crawling
through Alex's brain
leaving a fiery black track
like a lightning strike

the octopus?

no.
but it smelt of sea

as did Phoebe's skin
plastering to hers
deliciously

but now the creature's tentacles
are coldly electric

taking her away from the safe earth
of sex

taking her, dragging her now
in its mollusc-like beak,
to her fate of sea,
a cold alien sea

Europa.

Mango daiquiri

That last drink with Phoebe
was a mango daiquiri

drunk in the warm, fragrant dusk
of sea level

the rain was beating down
like a muffled drum

they had the bar
by the pool
almost to themselves

they were talking
in the languid spell
of their sweet potent drinks
about sweet nothing

She never

Phoebe never rang, wrote
nor replied to a few feeler
e-mails from Alex

red-raw longing
glowed
under their excruciating
Memory Lane flirting
like trapped lava

over the years
it had been
a lot easier for Alex
to hate Phoebe
than forget her.

Flames

She was kidding herself
to call Phoebe
an old flame

more an old wound
a dribbling smoulder
a humiliating confusion.

And Alex wearily knew
that conferences
were tar pits
for the restlessly married

which isn't you
her warm wedding ring
reassures her
with the welcome chain
of the domestic flame.

America—The Adjective

Phoebe at the podium
is so American.

Articulate.
Impossible to believe
she has a molecule
of stuttering humanity.

Territorial.
Her mind not only knows
but owns
the cosmos.

Vulgar.
Spruiking her quasars, her black holes
and galaxies
like Big Mac Specials.

Puritanical.
Fiddling
with the fussy little buttons
over her breasts.

Narcissistic.
Thighs
belly, breast and bum
gym-perfect.

Insular.
No mysteries left.
Phoebe, why bother looking out
the window?
Why bother looking at me?

Everywhere, everyone
is just waiting
to become America.

Even your mighty quasars
on the fiery edge of time
will learn to wear
their galaxy-gorging jets
base-bloody-ball
backwards.

Adultery

She's changed.
Older, paler.
Even—why are my eyes gobbling
her up!—brown spots
on her hands.

But it's Phoebe.
Still Phoebe.

I still shiver
in the icy gaze
of her pale clever eyes.

And my old desire wakes up
like a desiccated Martian
flood plain
sniffing a huge fresh flood.

What new germs
will her lightning strikes
spark
in my parched thin soil?

Does she have my room number?

Daniel. Daniel.

My husband's name
is no amulet
against this fever

this fever
that makes me fret and sweat

while my heart divides
and procreates.

Black water

Let my fears drown
as they slip under
the ice lid and fall
ripe for illumination
into this liquid warm
claustrophobia

where my eyes must smell
as I jet like a nautilus
into the panoramic unimaginable.

Two-pot screamer

It's not just
  being pissed

it's her
  being with her

it's my button

can't blame her
   too easy

she doesn't push it

I push her
   to push it

It Never Happened

Deliciously
   ill at ease
Alex sits in a hotel room
telling herself
It Never Happened

there is no need
   for self-recrimination
or counting her Daniel
   blessings

It Never Happened

Phoebe did not
   kiss her.
seriously. kiss her.

she remembers
it was a good cold
four hundred years
between supernovae

better to believe
    It Never Happened
than live and glow
    in that annihilating bang.

Driving to Venus

She's not driving
    like an icy comet
    burning up
to Phoebe

it's early morning
    serenely dark
she's driving to the airport
incandescently
    on too little sleep

there's a crisp silence
clearing her path
to the pale dark sky's
  only star.

Venus.
Wide-eyed lovely awake
    prodding her
        with love's luminescence.

Bugs and bitters

And when Alex gets home late
  stubbing her toe
    on guilt
      and heady satiation

she doesn't know
whether to wince
    or grin
      with sloppy idiotic pleasure

she's been downing
an alien bitters
  and its bugs are taking her
    over.

The Kraken sleepeth

In the abysmal depths of sleep
something quivers and stirs
on Alex's steaming ocean floor

let me be

Too driven by curiosity to ever
run cold
Alex's blood trembles in its tracks

turn it off

But her mind is too greedy
to give back the dark
and she holds the cruel beam steady

you've got what you want
my peace   this conversation

And something thrashes
to the surface

and leaves its message floating
rank in Alex's breath

> *remember where you found me*

Black holes gig

My heart is exploding.
In two days she'll be here.
In my city, in my blood
stream.

A fellowship at Melbourne Uni.

'A black holes gig'
she said laughing
over the phone.

And I feel my whole universe
squeeze and shrink
as it falls joyfully
in.

Never forget

Alex knows
she will never forget
how beautiful Phoebe looks
standing before a dark mirror
wrapped in a pale blue motel towel
looking back at her.

Alex notes everything.

Phoebe's long naked legs.
Her own cold feet in the cold sheets
wanting Phoebe to come back
and thaw them.
Her nipples still warmly moist
from Phoebe's tongue.
The drawn dusty curtains.
The ugly print
of a blue and yellow St Kilda.
Phoebe's eyes. Phoebe's eyes.

The beast

'It could just as easily
have been called
The Semen Way'
Phoebe tells me
in her sharp dirty way.

We're lying under a rug
somewhere
outside Ballarat
by a murmuring invisible river.

The Milky Way streaming
and sparkling over
our heads
is making me happily
bereft of smart competitive
metaphors.

'Milky? It's not a dear old moo cow
up there.
There's a beast, a real beast,
at the centre of our galaxy

but it's no domesticated pet.
It roars in gamma rays
from its black hole lair
of a million crushed suns.
And one day, babe,
all those pretty stars
blue, red and brindle
and all who sail on them
will pour down
its black gullet
and disappear forever.'

Snuggling into Phoebe's warm side
I grin at her horror story

nearby in the swampy smell
frogs are making a wonderful
racket.

The wonder

she must love me
she must love me
Alex's heart thumps
as Phoebe
   takes her hand
and holds it in the hollow
   between her breasts

with the last residue
     of adult restraint
Alex holds her silence
and lets the rapture
   in Phoebe's softly American
      spider voice
hold her in its spinning silk

'Astronomers are the chosen ones,
darling,
how can anyone go out at night
   look up
and not want to be one of us?

I wet myself once
  because I couldn't leave the telescope
   because I was looking back
      to the beginning of time.
I was looking at the real dragons, Alex,
quasars with blow-torch jets
   as long as three galaxies.
I love knowing
  what those monsters don't.

They're extinct.
Nothing survives.

You grow up the minute
you don't take this universe
   too seriously,
but the wonder, the gog-eyed wonder,
   never goes away.'

The hardy limpet

And then she picks my hand
off her chest
as if it were a clinging
stray.

I hear that old grunt
of restless boredom
and whatever closeness we had
is over.

But I'm still listening,
still hearing her whirring awe
still feeling the pressure
of her fingers.

I know why I love this
dazzling woman.

So what
she's as remote from my frailties
as her blazing quasars.

She makes me stand
in the breath of her hot hard
truths.

Marital sex

I am not lying in my enemy's
    arms.

Why am I heartsore
    for the sound and smell
        of a war in my bed?

Daniel's baby-soft curls
smell as dear as ever
  as he sucks my breasts.

Do I really want a whiff
    of sour wine
        and gunpowder,
an asteroid called Eros
    crashing through my roof?

Oxygen

'Oxygen'
  Phoebe chants
    like a smirking curse
'there won't be enough
    oxygen'

As always
she's right.

Europa's ice crust
  shutting out the sun
could be a coffin lid
for anything bigger
  than an anaerobic bug.

Oxygen.
And my mind bubbles
  into a blue aquarium,
    shining with gulping fish,
   alit like the translucent tail
      of a fluttery male sea horse
        his belly bulging with eggs.

Sun-rich water,
    and all its living loot.

While Phoebe's finned jibe
    cold-eyed and hungry
cruises Europa's black water
    hunting down
        all my vulnerable wonders.

Radiation

When
pushing back strands
of her hair straying
around her dangerous
quick-quipping mouth

kissing her
feeling her mouth open
like an anemone
under mine

when I flow to her
fast and shallow
like a channel
from a deep lagoon
frothing across to the sea

I have her intense attention.

It's only afterwards
wearily driving home
I feel my skin

flake away
in a leprous snowfall

as if I've strayed
and played
in Jupiter's radiation belt.

Romantic

Phoebe tells me
I'm such a romantic
I should be writing poetry
on purple paper
(would Daniel laugh harder
at the poetry or the paper?)

But, Phoebe says,
being romantic
is not cute or clever
for a female astronomer.

Phoebe has all the grim statistics
at her feminist fingertips
about the women
who chose a man
over the mission,
the appointment,
or telescope time.

Of course
lesbians like herself

could be the foolhardiest
romance junkies of all,
chucking hard-won careers
away on a whim, a fling,
a pretty face
in an exotic place

but not her not her

sure she likes me,
the wild starry talking
the great sex
and, oh yeah, the laughs

but. she was warning me.
come crunch time
she. Phoebe.
would be. without apology.
a man.

The jellyfish

In her husband's glass
through the finger-marked frost
Alex watches
a whirling jellyfish
dissolving slowly
in his wine

lovely
  translucent
    trapped

a clinking dead end.

wild surmise

Alex had long and ruefully
known
that only sensational astrophysical
discoveries
could make Phoebe really tremble

but she herself was still
reeling
from Phoebe's breaking into poetry
like a dry salt lake suddenly
spouting fresh water

'I'm staring
like Keats's *stout Cortez* staring
for the first time at the Pacific'
Phoebe had said
with wet flashing eyes

'I'm staring
at a great new ocean,
an invisible ocean
pulsing and repulsing

like a black high tide
through the universe

dark energy.
it exists, Alex,
this Hubble pic proves it.

look, this supernova
is just too damn bright

it proves the universe
is expanding,
but not steadily

gravity and my ocean
of dark energy
are fighting it out'

then Phoebe looked at Alex
with a wild surmise.

VOLCANOES

Daniel's Song

My wife reads the world
with a long-distance microscope.

How does she read me
squatting on her toes
pressing my kneecaps in?

My heart signals to her
like a colossal rapacious
alien
flashing frantically
from an overlooked moon.

oh darling oh my love
find me   find me

a green Thought in a green Shade

My garden is not Paradise
but it's a small-time Eden
of sorts.

And like Marvell
I can revel in its
green embrace
without missing its Mistress
too unbearably much.

Is he right in arguing
with such lusciously lonely
metaphysical wit
that it's best
to wander solitary?

Do any of us really
have much choice?

The marvel of a ripening lemon
can't be shared any better
than the bone-scratching terror
of cancer.

We're all alone.

Perhaps it's the only way
to really feel
your own pulse
of green poetry.

Hanging Rock

Dawdling behind his wife
through the clefts of damp
eerie smelling rocks
Daniel thinks enviously
of Oedipus,
ground to his life's halt
at Colonus,
when the earth gently opened
beneath his feet.

Panting a little
behind his wife's long
restless stride,
Daniel remembers walks
when they jostled shoulders
on narrow bush tracks
deliriously together
never thinking
to walk in single file.

How long ago?
five years
or ten?

Now a gang of acned
stomping yobs
suddenly, like a pipe
gushing raw sewage,
bursts down
the path

'They're everywhere'
Daniel snarls
like a cornered old dog
'the dickbrains.
they're winning.'

Alex turns around
she's glowing eyes
all laughing lava

'We're standing on
an old volcano, darling'

a zigzagging flash
of crimson rosellas
erupts over their heads

'and volcanoes always
have the last word.'

The cradle

Alex turns over and over
in her hot grabby mind
the images from the Pilbara rocks
Rachel Epstein, microbiologist
and good friend,
blew up for her.

Three-billion-year-old threads.
Delicate skeletons.
Sulfur guzzling microbes
from an ancient thermal spring
when the young earth seethed
and boiled.

Life was spawned in Hell.
Jubilant
it thrived and multiplied
and danced
in the scalding
stench.

like love

Alex's breasts prickle

What was mewling
what was crying out
from the fiery cold cradle
of Europa
to suck her milk?

The kiss of bacteria

'If I kissed you properly
on the mouth'
Rachel speculates
  with sexless wonder
staring with her unblinking scientific
    gaze
at Alex's lips
'we'd make such an interesting
    bacterial swab together'

Alex suddenly imagines
  their kiss
    sliced into an exquisitely tiny
      section
        for Rachel's electron microscope

and their unlikely pash
 magnified half a million times
into the sinister unsentimental geometry
  of Rachel's world, the real world—
        black-hearted rods and spheres.

Under the ice

Holding ice
in your bare hand
hurts

but Alex is an ice
fanatic

her burning hands trembling
compulsively over her computer keys
as they scan Europa
every day for evidence
of ice volcanoes.

Just as she is longing
for evidence
of Phoebe's spectacular eruptions—

what is really under her ice?
what wriggling wonder
would spurt one day
from under Phoebe's ice-hard
eyes
 and splash all over Alex?

Oh happy day
when her heart's sky
burns and burns
with the searing display
 of her two most precious moons
    generously erupting!

Prickling

Daniel curls around me
soft as a mollusc
in his sleep

insomnia prickles like a sea urchin
and grows
into a toothache
of Phoebe's mouth
dissolving into mine

I try to shut
this worn old porn off
and instead
send my mind
as a submersible
to Europa

let me dream
clusters of tube worms
growing like Medusa hair
into white curlers

let me gag on a cloud
of giant squid's ink

anything
but abducting myself
on a sterile fantasy
mindlessly masturbating
on a woman
who despises me.

Pretty rats

'What are you?'
 Phoebe asks
  taking Alex's long blazing face
   in her hand

'are you just a wife, honey,
 a very nice man's philandering wife?'
  then kisses Alex
   seriously slowly

'despite having the loveliest mouth
  in the world
you make a shit-awful lesbian, Alex,
I'd be a fool
to get too fond of you,
if she wasn't so ugly
 your dyke pal, Rachel,
  would be a much smarter
bet'

enjoying the closeness
 of Phoebe's breath and lips
Alex plays along

'Rachel's asexual, not a lesbian,
　I've only ever known her
　　　to cuddle up
　　　　with her pet rat, Shigella,
　　　　　mind you,
　　　　　　he's a very pretty rat'

'What are you then?'
Phoebe croons stroking
　Alex's dark fine brows
'what are you?'

Alex closes her eyes
　　trembling into the caress
anything you fancy
your exploding star.
your pygmy hippopotamus.
　anything. anything. you fancy

Black smokers

I can withstand
this.

Black smokers
come and go.

And their colonies
of sulfur glutton bacteria
and heat junkie worms
move on.

I can withstand
her.

Let me be an iron-deaf
seabed
that will not fold
at the hot lick of her voice

not crack
at the magma push
of her touch

not let her
thermal boiling memory poison
through.

Dark matter

Phoebe knows how
to make my Europan microbe
look ordinary

the Are We Alone debate
only makes her jeer
'I like being alone'

my lover is a more ambitious hunter,
her prey
the universe's invisible guts
dark matter
that neither emits nor absorbs
ordinary light

gravity
its only spoor.

Towards its mystery
towards its maw
Phoebe is willingly,
almost wantonly,
drawn.

When Venus erupted

Tonight Venus is tauntingly
beautiful
as she drops from the lilac
twilight sky
into my glass of wine

I'm drinking too much, Phoebe

my stomach just rains acid
when it tries to digest you.

When Venus erupted
she was smothered in lava
when Venus erupted
all her oceans boiled away

did she harbour life?
did she turn fierily sterile
to spite herself?

All affairs are like this.

You choke on your own run-away
gases.
You die
of excitement.

Invitation to the abyss

Rachel swats the invitation
at my face

'we're off to the ball
on the East Pacific Rise
ocean floor,
eight hours cramped together
in a sub, Alex'

A feast on the gushing abyss.
gobbling at incredible pressure
my favourite party food—
life at its most exotic unlikely.

Time out.
Precious and fantastic.
From Daniel's caressing
nudging attentiveness.
And Phoebe's offhand
lust.

Rapture of the Deep

The submersible is sinking
through the layers
of sea,
like a brave roving thought
sinking to the bottom
of a black dream.

Rachel is noisily watching
the silent deep water
fireworks,
as translucent killers
flash blue and red X rays
for mates or meat.

While Alex is impatiently waiting
for euphoria,
even a dangerous narcosis,
to kick in.

Black and hot and cold

Rachel's excited oxygen-greedy
breath
smells of peanuts

'we're here   we're here'

Alex's long left leg
is cramping

the tiny sub's window
is black.

Before the frail light
is switched dimly on,
before her own eyes
can gorge,
Alex's mind rips and splits
like the ocean floor

and black lava bubbles
rear up
in a hiss of challenge

of life about to be spawned
in her own boiling cold dark.

Real

A white octopus appears suddenly
like a tentacled ghost
at the window

Alex imagines her own hand
mulched by the pressure
as she reaches out
to touch it.

Underneath them
bacteria blanket the rocks
like a dark dawn
glittering with frost

but Alex won't wake up
and crow

she leaves the breathless
gush
to Rachel.

And even the pearly worms
draped over the stones
like strands of spaghetti
only remind her of the pasta
she left congealing in cold tasteless
white sauce
the last time she saw Phoebe.

'Even the shrimps are blind
down here'
Rachel murmurs
'it's a different kind of sensitivity
that matters'

sensitivity
Alex's skin crawls
with yearning

and she imagines putting her face
under the rock pipe
spitting hot sulfurous water
and giving her skin something
real
to agonise over.

The Tube Worm Pillar

The fat red-plumed tube worms
wave in the sub's face
like a hundred fluttering dicks.

Alex shifts in her seat
as her cunt prickles
mechanically responding
as if to a surreal porn flick.

Why does she slobber over
pricks on the screen
more than the one in her bed?

Why do these swaying
fleshy stalks
so arouse her?

Poor old Daniel
not even competition
for the sulfur-stinking
sprogs
of the sexy, salty sea.

The solar wind

On the pitch-black ocean floor
Phoebe was still battering
Alex's psychic atmosphere

while Rachel's tiny, small-mouthed
face,
impersonating a happy *Pompeii* worm
poking out of its tube,
was talking about the latest
black smoker fashion statement
'bacterial shaggy coats'.

Alex felt like the surface of Mercury,
coatless in its scorching orbit,
irradiated beyond rescue.

Death and Destruction

in the abyss   over the edge
she can't wait
  a knot
  unravelling in her gut

her eyes anticipate
a wild eerie overload

the sub's puny headlights
switch on
and milkily sweep
the ocean floor

but
  she blinks
but
  there's nothing
but
black charred
  nothing

the water has killed
everything
like black suffocating oil

the water hates life
the seafloor grins
black and glassy

the pilot is enjoying himself
rubbing their noses in it
the little sub lingers
rubbernecking
over the steaming
lifeless wreck

'a new volcano's handiwork'
he says proudly

'they giveth   they taketh away'
Rachel's breath erupts
awesomely in Alex's ear.

Going dead boat

The submersible settles on the seafloor
and the smirking pilot
shuts down all systems

'we call it
  going dead boat'

his voice drifts thin
  in the pounding silence

and a kind of DTs settles on me
as I see through the pitch black
the sides of the sub
sweating worms

and even without Rachel's
hot dry hand clutching mine
I know everything
    steel   rock   water

is alive
    and teeming beyond my
        endurance

Mister Hyde

Phoebe glances at Rachel's worm
photos from the vents
and shuddering
   pushes them away

'Jesus, Alex, imagine those
   repulsive things
a thousand times bigger
just waiting for your meddling naiveté
   down in the Europan mud.'

Her fear is a show of sexy weakness
and makes me know
  we'll be going to bed soon
    and sets off my own
  unfightable quivering.

I'd be happy,
  I tell her,
    drifting into her eyes,
to find a few cute bugs

'Bullshit.
You're just another Doctor Jekyll
poking, prying
   and hoping.

Christ knows what toxic Mister Hyde
your blundering ice probe could find
   and free.'

Singularity

Is the point where Phoebe has
infinite power.

I am dead. While watching myself
fall towards her.

Stripped to subatomic particles
I am dead. But faster than the speed
of light.

I moan *I am dead*. Through the infinitely hot
point of no return.

The War of the Worlds

no one would have believed
no one gave a thought

Did Alex ever believe
    give a thought
to lying in the oily tentacles
    of a mesmerising Martian?

across the gulf of space
intellects vast and cool
and unsympathetic

Across the gulf of Phoebe's bed
  two nauseating eyes regard Alex
    with a vast and cool
      and unsympathetic intelligence

Elwood Beach

This morning, after falling through
the seven heavens of Li Po's
wine and waterfall poetry,
Daniel takes a falling leaf
 from the poet's book,
    and gorging on idleness
gulps down the sunny breeze
   whiffy with rotting seaweed
     and white-crested lapping
         memory.

Two glittering demons stroll
towards him,
his old self with Alex,
   hand in hand.

He shields his eyes
  from the glare
of their happiness
and tranquilly
   lets their distant-past bliss
      wash over him.

He is not here
    to go crazy.

Dogshit on the path.
Its swarming stink
    no heart-hurting phantom.

Nothing like fresh dogshit
to make the present
    punch back.

Greasy Joe's

Why does Memory Lane
never lose the sizzling savour
of junk food?

Chips and hamburgers.
Greasy fingers.
Steamy windows.
Parked by a frothing
St Kilda Beach in winter.
That sweet old pressure
   against the zipper.

Oh Alex.

And so I find myself hooked
and drifting through the door
towards that siren smell
of Greasy Joe's—
fug, beer and burgers.

I have a quiet but urgent dream
of a piled plate, a schooner,

a spot of early Yeats
and a romantic glutton's peace.

Am I
  choking on yellow gas
    and now seeing
      devils?

Alex and ... who?
Some sharp-faced
bitch
   holding my wife's hands.

My devils
  haven't seen me.
They only see,
  only bedazzle,
    each other.

Am I in Hell?
  or the most noxious terrace
    of Purgatory
where you grin and sing and bear
it

    because why?
        you'll learn to love it.
          your own holy poison.

Oh Alex.
I've mushed
into grey cold slop
sloshing itself tidily
out the door
to the filthy street.

    Right out of your fucking way.

Living with it

caught in a grey cloud
  I can't rain
caught on Punt Road
  I can't crash

there is oyster grit
  in my eye

it's my wife's shattered
  aphrodisiac

should I weep it away
  or live with it
    and go blind?

Diagnosis

The diagnosis is obvious
and, like cancer, the question
is the same
   how long have I got?

Of course there are other questions
blooming like blue-green algae
in the river of my happily meandering
marriage
   how long have you been seeing her?
   do you like her cunt better than my cock?

Or maybe I need a second opinion.
A mate to tell me I'm seeing things,
it's benign
   just two old girlfriends catching up.

But I don't have mates
like that any more.
My last few years have been
furiously spent, trying not
to gut Brian Howard slowly

with a rusty fishing knife,
>   trying to keep my job.

Not to mention the usual blokey
laziness
>   *my wife's my best friend*
christ knows she's not
>   when did we last forget the time
>   just talking?

The diagnosis is clear.
My marriage is cactus.

This is my Gallipoli.
Just hit the beach shooting.

Virus

She must be miserable,
she's not throwing her coffee down
like her throat's made of asbestos,
instead she's staring at it
as if I've just poured her a cup
   of hot poison.

If I were a stronger
   better man
I'd bring this whole unsaid mess
   to the boil
      and make her drink it.

I sip my coffee
  joylessly
(when did I last enjoy anything?)
and ask about her work.

She shrugs

'sometimes it feels
like I've got herpes,

it lives dormant
in my nerves
then tingles
and burns to the surface
in itching little ulcers,
then it goes away again
but there's no cure, Daniel,
I've got it for life'

we're both laughing
   joylessly
we both know
she's not talking
about Europa.

Extremophiles

I can't read Plath any more.

But she's still the only poet
my wife reads
   or knows.

Other poets I've urged on her
are 'crap' or 'boring'.

So why does Plath escape
my wife's exacting critique?

Alex just laughs
'Sylvia's an extremophile'

What does she mean?
Thermal vent poetry?
Writhing curses
  stinking of sulfur?

Or is Plath just the smelly black music
playing behind

my wife's feeding frenzy
on her secret girlfriend's bubbling
  germs?

If my wife can only love
the boiling extreme
  she can't
    of her own willing accord
      love me

THE DARK WOOD

Cold (1)

How can she live
such a cold life?

Even her working thoughts
swarm and swim
through a dead cold universe.

What kind of creature
thrives on the cold?

Maybe Phoebe is the germ
I'll discover
when I pick Europa's
ice-jammed lock

and like the swooning
mug maiden
I've invited my own
infectious vampire in.

Cold (2)

How can she live
such a cold life
my distant wife?

I watch her
like I watch
the cold August wind
tossing
the blossoming pink
magnolia tree.

I watch her
because frozen sea
or blown early spring bloom
she's precious to me.

Cider

All it takes is one delicious sip.

And he floats apple-cider sweetly
back
into the twentieth century.

He tastes every note
of the 60s and 70s
as his forty-nine-year-old bones creak
blissfully along
to the pub's archaic jukebox.

And he imagines falling in love
with his wife again
where every raven
on every telegraph pole
becomes blue–black shimmering
beautiful
and frilled with significance

where music and grog
weave a glassy green wave

swelling over the sandbar
to take him salt-faced
and joyful
into the remembering
long white beach of her.

Another sip
his mouth fills with cider poetry.
And he can smell the apple-blossom
in an ecstatic scrap of Sappho.

He presses his friendly wet male nose
against the glass of that ancient lesbian's
bittersweet aching blundering bliss
for one sweetly sodden moment.

Until a big sour burp wakes him up
to just another
whingeing old dyke.

Tedious, tedious Sappho
wringing her inky hands
on another lilac twilight
under her pronged toxic evening star

praying pleading
yet bloody again
to lie in some cold girl's
arms

just like his wife.

Just like his wife
swigging on her twenty-first century
strychnine
of sterile planets
and parching women.

Malaise

Rock'n'roll is dead.

There's an endless mid 70s
    guitar solo
boring, twanging on
    and on and on
        in me.

Is this stale
  no-talent noise
    telling me something?

I'm your requiem, pal.
Move over. Go quietly.
Drop dead.

Daniel's view

My inner eye
is shuddering
at the view

but is trying to let
me down gently

it's nothing, mate,
just a garden variety
gut ache

but I know
there's a monster
on the march

whose lumps are growing
into a thorny randy parasite
eyeing me
relentlessly off.

Living organism

Daniel tells Alex
what the doctor said

and she thinks
of taking his hand

but doesn't.

Instead she concentrates
on not fainting

she's horrified at herself

it's not as if he's bleeding
all over her.

He's his usual
eloquently contained self

just white-faced.

Her brave frightened
man

is not a computer-animated
proto-trilobite

or an extraterrestrial
roving probe
bristling with immortal
intelligence.

He's a complex vulnerable
living organism

that's faltering
and turning fatally
on itself

and,
forget the human miracle
of the amazing neural galaxy
in his skull,
beyond her help.

Hospital

What poet will accompany me
to hospital?

Cavafy?

No. I'm too terrified
for a neo-pagan poof's
uncomforting meditations
on falling on your sword,
with stiff upper lip
twitching to a divine music
as the gods pull up their pegs . . .

Dickinson?

No. She always insists
like a kind of spinster Lear
that you live in the prickling
lace-work
of her lunaticking storms.

Keats?

No. His whingeing is too
lush
and no hospital bed can bear
that many anaesthetising
flowers.

Oh God.
I'm so frightened.

My coffee. My beloved
Melbourne libation
just tastes of ether.

But when I sleep
when I sleep
to be cut open
to be cut to raw and bloody pieces
I will wake to pain
and catheters.

To banal strangers.
The callous good cheer
of surgeons.

Of course.
I will take Dante.

Dante and I will weep
together
as the leopard and the lion
and the gaunt grey wolf
all take their bite
and the Dark Wood
tangles us together
in a brotherhood
of shivering necessity.

Oh Dante.
Wrap me close
in your warm brave eloquence.

Marlowe

But it is Marlowe
who comforts me best
in this gnawing distress
of post-operative chemo.

Marlowe, my sweetly fiendish cat,
whose fragrant beauty
could launch a thousand
I-want-to-live
ships.

My lovely boy.

Not the swaggering pederast
poet
dying with a dagger
in his recklessly brazen atheist
eye.

My blue Burmese
lying like a lover
in my arms

purring with green eyes shut
as if my love
is a flickering fire, a warm mouse.

And then he gets
sick of that, sick of me
and bites.

If only my wife,
waiting on me anxious,
guilty
hand and bloody foot,
could love me
as blissfully, as truthfully,
as my cat.

Bald

This look
is the bald truth.

I have cancer.
I'm on chemo.
My hair has fallen out.

The mirror
in its usual cruel glassy drawl
tells me the look
does nothing for me.

Wispy fuzz. A few skull warts.
And my eyes look lost.
Lost their warrior lustre.

My curls were clearly
my balls.

Cancer is my Delilah
shearing me unmanning me
while I dozed my days away

slobbering in the seductive lap
of my body's own fake wellbeing.

You never know from where
your enemies will spring.

Mine, the deadliest,
came with a razor
from within.

Resistance

I am resisting
the slow cold descent
into Hell.

I don't ask my doctor
how long have I got?
I don't ask Alex
who are you seeing?

I'm enjoying
hatching
the red flower-spiders
on my new grevillea

and hope one
will jump on me
like a benign funnel-web
and change my luck.

Most comforting of all
I'm sleeping in
with my old mate Dante

and holding his vibrating hand.

Breakfast

It's strange the scraps
of crap you pick up—

bits and pieces
of smart-arse nothing
like cramming
for a game show
that holds no surprises
or prizes.

Am I getting nastier?

Or is cancer
the excuse I've always
been looking for?

No matter how dreadful
I feel
or how much Alex tries
to notice or care
there's always this
little hum

coming off her
like a nauseating odour
of happiness.

Well, this morning
over a breakfast,
that will sit in my constipated
gut
like concrete,
I will tell her
what I've just read
christ-knows-where
about her Giordano Bruno
astrobiology's Head Martyr—

they burnt him
for not acknowledging
the divinity of Jesus

not, my deluded love,
for waving the extraterrestrial
flag

he was just another
crazy heretic mug
dying in agony
for a medieval
hair-splitting pointless
nothing.

That might just smother
for a moment
the hum
of her horrible pity.

The corporate world

Daniel doesn't hesitate
crossing the threshold
of Alex's study

he trembles a little
standing in her dusty
charged space

and gripes
with envy
at its smell of creative
industry.

He flicks
at her astronomy calendar
baring his teeth
at Europa

'you fucking nothing
of a grubby golf ball'

But stopping at
the floating blue jewel
of Earth
he rubs his bony
unshaved jaw
and shudders

lucky lucky Alex

the gorgeous freedom
to limitlessly itch
her own thoughts

let her try
sublime floating in black
fertile space
one whole day
in his corporate world
of the user-pays university

let her try
to mentally melt
the ice cap of her stubborn moon
while admin e-mail

nags and bites
like sandflies

that blue dot jewel
would snap in her fingers
like a junk plastic heart
listening to one more
slack-arse illiterate
student
demanding a Distinction
for one more scrap
of crapulous cyberfiction
or worse
yet another
lazy dead poem.

Maybe it had given him cancer,
giving in
giving up
giving the little fuckers
what they insisted their money
had bought them.

Meanwhile
he had contempt, chemo
and his wife's e-mail password . . .

while lucky lucky Alex
was out
fucking
the stars.

Infidelity by e-mail

Christ, she's stupid.

Daniel can't believe
his wife's password
is really *Europa*.

For a moment he trickles
reluctance.

Maybe it shows
she has nothing to hide.

Or thinks he's
fucking stupid.

Europa   Europa

He'll blast that moon
to mush.

Or is Europa
her only mistress?

He could live with that.
You can't fuck ice.

But within seconds
he's howling for ice
with the screaming need
of a burns victim.

Her Inbox
is her trysting love nest.

Her stink-hole.

The endearments crawl
into Daniel's eyes
like maggots.

But from under the scalding fug
one name surfaces
and floats
like a big black turd
that will never flush away.

Phoebe.

First cigarette

Was the chemo killing
his fire
rather than fighting his tumour?

Was coming into work
a mistake?

His computer screen
an unappetising nag
of unanswered e-mail.

fuck off everyone
I've got cancer

Boring voices
in the corridor,
Daniel sighs
and drags himself up
to shut the door

it makes a satisfying
fuck-off bang

he shuts down his computer
and breathes in
silence

and contemplates again,
like his tongue obsessively
poking a new ulcer,
the state of his marriage.

He tries to remember
the smell of his wife's hair,
her head snuggling
into his shoulder in bed
while she was dozing
off to sleep

now she just made
his shoulder ache
but he was too lonely
or paralysed
to shove her off.

There was something
charmless

about his wife's latest
infidelity

no grand passion
just a dog (a stupid bitch)
returning to the vomit
of an addictive old girlfriend

the kiss, root n' tell
of their panting e-mail.

Daniel's hands shake
then clench

today, right now,
he was going to have
his first cigarette
in eleven years.

Alex wasn't the only one
who liked to suck
what was bad for her.

Prayer

What would Larkin say
in his sour-quatrain perfect
way
about how Brian Howard
orders his coffee?

Macchiato.
With his crooked pinkie
little jug of hot milk
on the side.

And how much
grim and nasty Philip
would enjoy
this grey bleak day,
spiced and sprinkled with
the waiter's junkie pallor
and Brian Howard's corporate
logorrhoea.

Today I don't even have
the eloquence
of sycophancy.

Nor the flash-flood fight
left to say

mate, I just want to fail
the fucking lot of them

Just a prayer.
A simple prayer
as my own coffee bubbles
unfriendly
under the waistband of my saggy
jocks.

I pray for Brian Howard
to die.
now.
without benefit
of morphine or clergy.

I pray for my own repulsive
present
to depart and cease.

That's all.
Like the true Larkin hero,
oh so creepy,
I've never dared to be greedy.

There's always one

There's always one.

And this one
   a woman of course
Liz Monday
 my age
   and looking every minute of it
despite the slash
   of loud pink lipstick.

And why is she more work
   than the rest of the class
slapped together?
   Dear dumb little things
who'd root their mothers
   for a good mark.

Why does Liz fucking Monday
   lie
that she's read every single book
   ever aborted
let alone published?

'120 Days of Sodom?'
   I tried calling her bluff

she didn't even stop rustling
   her infernally noisy notes

'twice'
   she replied
'the second time in the original
   Italian'

Gotcha!

But I refrained
  from rustling my own notes
and pompously correcting her
   'the Marquis de Sade wrote
     in *French*, Liz'

I'm finally learning.

Instead I've been giving her
   her head
letting her talk at ignorant length
   about books she's never read

and even better
   her own masterpieces
the intricate hard labour
   behind every flat-footed
boring word

while the rest of the class
   is too comatose
to challenge me, her,
   or care.

But one day Liz Monday
   will wake up
out of her garrulous conceited
   torpor
and know she's been got at

and then
   and only then
she'll pen
   her best work, her passionate
tour de force

a letter to Brian Howard
   her match in this world
and christ knows the next
   accusing me of what?

perfidious
   politically incorrect
scorn?

no.
   she'll stick to this age's
favourite script.

she'll tell Brian
   I've been harassing her
sexually harassing her.

My haemorrhoids

Tonight I'm counting
my haemorrhoids.

One.
My wife on television.
All intense charisma
and big brown eyes.
Talking with sexy jokes
about the sensual sex life
of an octopus alien.

I burp
aiming my stubbie at the screen
she's fucking boring at home!

Two.
Brian Howard on the phone.
His voice flat and dry
sticking up my nose like dried
snot.
Telling me, not asking,
to write a report

justifying to a departmental cost-cutting
committee
the continuing value of my course
on Romantic Poetry.

I'm teaching the little bastards
how to write commercially viable
Valentine's Day cards
and, besides,
it's keeping me alive, Brian

Three.
And last.
Myself unsuccessfully
on the dunny.
All that codeine turning me
into catastrophically constipated Coleridge
without the visionary consolations.

Oh, dear STC, straining painfully
alongside of me
wouldn't you swap your demon lover
for the explosive gift
of a decent shit?

The last time

There was nothing exceptional
about the last time
Alex saw Phoebe.

They talked about their work.
Alex took Phoebe's hand.
They both drank too much
too quickly.

But Alex remembered,
when she was going over
the evening
just one more nerve-aching
time,
that Phoebe had skirted her mouth
as if it were radioactive.

For the first and last time
Phoebe had kissed her
goodbye
on the cheek.

Cracks

She has decided to go with a guess.

The Europan cracks
   are habitats
flushed with titanic tides
oxygenated, warm enough,
   it would be a struggle
   but what isn't?

The sulfur deposits
   were a lurid tease,
just puffing Io polluting
   the place.

But the cracks. the cracks.
cracked like crazy
   cracked like checking her e-mail
     three hundred times a day
       allowing Phoebe to be her Io
         polluting her peace.

She wishes she were frozen solid.
And something stiff in her
would crack and buckle
and let the mystery
melt through.

The red shifting lover

Phoebe won't give me
the drama
　or the grace
of a break-up scene

it's like perpetual
cold coffee
　a horrible cheat
and nothing
to burn my mouth on

but the scorching freeze
of her answering machine.

Cold Turkey

It was like a fiendish flu.
A flu with the grip
of an anaconda.

Nothing
was giving Alex
relief, reprieve
or pleasure.

Even Europa was freezing
her out—
an iced-up chest jammed
terminally against her.

But it was her body's
loss
that was truly
torturing her.

It refused to ache
quietly.

mutely mourning
to its hurt self.

It raked at her.
It screeched, howled
and screamed.

For Phoebe.
For Phoebe's raging return.

At any cost.

My own skin

I'm back
  in my own grey skin.

Has everything become
  terribly simple?

Nothing a drink, a laugh
  and a sexy video
    can't fix?

Daniel and I
  treating each other
    like convalescing friends.

We've even taken up smoking
    again.

At our most tenderly intimate
  when his hand, or mine,
    shakes
      lighting the other's cigarette.

poetry makes nothing happen

as it happens, Auden, my dear,
today you're right

nothing is happening

no poem will water my garden
or
make my wife fancy me
or
thread health's good oil
through my grinding gears

nothing is happening

you must have known days like this
when Kallman was drunk and impossible
when everything you touched
felt filthy

and your poems, unlucky bugger,
tipped out their ash and singeing embers
on your ugly clever head

and nothing happened

except you smelt
like something nasty
slowly burning.

Honeyeaters (1)

When you're fucked
take an old pleasure
and dive into it.

Today the honeyeaters
darting through the branches
of the apricot tree
are an empty swimming pool.

They don't even give me
a metaphor to swim in.

Just yapping little grey birds.

I can't blame cancer.
We're growing together
like an exhausted marriage.

Is it because I wanted to chain Alex
to her chair last night
and make her watch
really watch
this abused old working elephant's distress?

Because it was hurting me
like a blunt needle jabbed in
I wanted it to hurt her

look you bitch look
what's happening to life
on your own planet

she was smiling
smiling to herself   not watching
the elephant's huge side
heaving with pain

her mind and heart
millions of miles away,
from me, the elephant
and the bloody TV,
chip chip chipping
at her dead little moon.

Click

I remember

there was a magnificent tree
through the dusty window
framing your glinting head

a giant gum
flaunting pink blossoms
swaying
like a showy dancer
waltzing by himself

when I knew
really knew, Phoebe,
you had never liked me.

Your back, as always,
to the view

your eyes
clicking over me
like a probe

processing images
from an insignificant moon
that holds no surprises.

Charged particles

Over breakfast
Alex is bombarding Daniel

'I love Jupiter
she just keeps making things
happen

her gravitational pull
is so sexy,
she gives the volcanoes on Io
the biggest and best
orgasms in the solar system

but it's her big-time radiation
that really turns me on.
Oh, her magnetic field
slams the ice of Europa
with charged particles
that can stir things up
like right-on-target sperm.
Europa could be pregnant, Daniel.'

Pregnant?
Daniel can't remember
which of them it was
who didn't want children

too late now.
christ knows what the chemo
was doing to his sperm count,
and when was the last time
he and Alex had sex anyway?

Pregnant?
Wasn't Alex nearly menopausal?

Maybe she could spend
the rest of her life
orbiting her pin-up Jupiter
and wait for those right-on-target
charged particles
to slam into her.

But wasn't Jupiter,
in nonsensical Alex-speak,
female?

Wouldn't it be just like Alex
to not only have the biggest and best
orgasms in the solar system
but then triumphantly trounce logic
and have a giant woman planet's baby?

Daniel's head
is aching horribly.

He wants to scream at his wife
and fall blubbering into his muesli.

Instead he waits for her
to shut up and notice, for her
to get to her bloody feet
come over
    and for the first time in a very long while
        touch him.

The Suicides' Wood

Dante, give me some credit.
I have not made my house
my gallows.

I don't hoard pills.

Nor does every fork
quivering in my hand
seek a faulty plug.

I'm eking out every moment
like a greedy kid spinning out
a bag of lollies.

I don't even know
when I'll be down
to my last musk stick.

Dante, give me some credit.
I'm growing tomatoes.
I'm smelling the rain.

I'm wearing my wife's
elsewhere itch.

Come what may.
Come what circle you find my soul
banqueting or anguishing.
I will not be your pitiful thornbush.

And my spirit will never
break away
black, bleeding and blubbering
in your sweet poet's
compassionate hand.

Mediocrity

There's something deafening
about mediocrity.

Today it's like
a tinnitus ringing
in my ears.

Grinding through the celebrity bullshit
magazines
in the dentist's waiting room
the ringing was torture.

I'm a failed academic.
A dinosaur humanist.
A cancer-ridden fucking joke
squeezing friendly old poems
for the juicy bits.

Alex, my bright distant darling,
I am your boring satellite
your minor planet

your unnamed moon
your black asteroid

with troglodyte habits
bad teeth
  and the great struggling crippled nothing
    of the mediocre
       to offer.

The Circle of the Lustful

Why does Dante
comfort me so much
in this long distress?

Dante doesn't ask
for ice-thin stoicism,
his silly scared poet
weeps buckets
in front of nice Virgil.

This afternoon
I can't read

like a sticky sick kid
I'm looking at pictures

Blake's Dante

letting myself
linger
  enviously

over the Circle
 of the Lustful

Blake's Centrefold

until its whirling lovers
 grab and grow
  in my aching gut
   like panting tumours.

Her kiss

Which lightning bolt
seared through me more?

Her kiss
  or his cancer?

After both
I smelt burnt.

But it was the soft sear
  of her mouth
that stood me on my tail
  alive   alive

like a parched fish
  pleading for electrocution
in a thunderstorm.

Exquisite cholera

Alex is only slightly drunk
half-listening to Rachel's
enthralled afternoon's lab work

'Have you ever really looked
at the cholera bug?
it is so exquisite'

maybe it's the trigger
exquisite
maybe it's a memory neuron
with a sudden hit of alcohol
releasing its goodies
with a rush of groggy generosity

because there
in her heart's eye
stands Phoebe

not in those fragments
that had tormented Alex

when she was trying
to go back to sleep

not just an aroused nipple
or a swollen mouth
or a whisper

it's Phoebe
in *exquisite* clarity
down to her white shirt
and favourite jeans
and nicotine-stained finger

and her face
sharp as glass
the merciless colour of her eyes
and the sometimes self-conscious pout
of her mouth

she's looking straight at Alex
aware of her
as if nothing else in the world
existed or mattered

Alex shudders

it must mean something
she must go home
and wait by the phone

'Why does everyone go green
and quiet
when I talk about cholera?'

Alex raises her glass to Rachel
and lets out a long passionate
breath

'To cholera!'

Calamari

My wife gives her
blatantly impatient sigh
explaining to Brian Howard
and his bloody horrible wife, Joanne,
why she doesn't eat calamari

don't bother, darling
I think
feeling a strange fresh solidarity
with my Alex
don't bother   just don't fucking bother

but she always does
even with dead-souled pricks
and stupid sneering bitches

this pair of fuckers
would eat their own kids
if you crumbed them nicely

I'm talking to her in my head
with more energetic love
than I've felt for months

while my mouth wears
the grim sloppy smile
of a gutless deadshit
taking his boss out
and fighting, every inch of the meal,
the urge to look at his watch

don't tell them
how you marvel at the octopus

tell me instead
about its large amazing brain
that flummoxes you
in a short-lived mollusc

tell me again, darling,
tell me again
the time you saw one
lurking in a rock pool
until it jetted away
in a huff of pink

the only animal
that really shows its feelings,
you joked

don't bother showing yours, my love,
to this pair . . .

Brian guffaws crunching
on his calamari rings,
Joanne makes a show
of shuddering

and some infinity of torture
later
I take out my credit card.

The partial eclipse

Through her binoculars
one side of the glowing moon
is blotched
with dark mossy seas

she lets her fancy
dog-paddle
before her gaze shifts
to the black egg eclipse

and yielding to the invitation
of all shadows
she hatches monsters

trembling
before she pulls her pieces together
to face her husband.

You must

you must change your life

I heard you, Rilke,
loud and clear and
  contemptuous

you must
  what? tell her.
    what?
when she comes in
from mooning over
  that dead yellow rock
tell her.

you must
  say.
you hate her with all your.
    what?

you must
  cut to the fucking chase
    for once in your dithering
      academic life

treat it like an illness.
   the Greek poets knew.
      like she's running a mortal fever.
oh christ, if only she'd die.
        did the Greeks know about hatred
            too?

give that woman up.
   or I'll kill you.

oh she won't believe her gentle
   Daniel
said that
   not Daniel
     with his balls dangling from his apron
as he cooks the great woman's
dinner

you must
   stand by me, Rilke.

Daniel's angel

Daniel paces the floor
like Rilke himself
on the battlements of Duino
an ecstatic lightning rod
buffeted in a gale, filling with poems
from his angel's storming mouth

and likewise
Daniel's angel paces with him
giving him a fluency
that if he could just stop
for one rapt second
would astonish him

but this is not inspired art
or a performance
he is fighting for his wife

and the words—
(is this why poetry and love
smelt together
with such seamless heat?)—
his words

reach out to Alex
and hold her in a loving grip
way beyond any strength
Daniel thought he had

at the back of his mind
he tells himself
to remember this flood
to remember the generosity
of his angel

'Daniel. darling.'

he stops
in the middle of the unswept floor
and tries to hear his wife
over the unangelic banging
of his heart

'You don't have to put yourself
through this.
it's all over.
she's gone.
gone.
back to Hawaii'

Daniel's angel exits
like a terrible Elvis movie
in a gurgle of blue lagooning shirts
and daggy surfboards

'Hawaii?'
he shakes his head
'Hawaii?'

'Remember?'
Alex gulps
'biggest and best telescopes
in the world.
biggest and best look
at the universe'

'Beats looking at you, eh?'
Daniel says with savagery

and knows his angel
has gone
and his own bitter sour self
is back
and swinging.

Worms

Be careful what you pray for.

Her head had been a can of worms
all year.

On some days she and Rachel
talked nothing but worms.

Giant tube worms stuffed like sausages
with bacteria.
Ice-happy worms burrowing into mounds
of methane.

She and Rachel had lived
like cheery *Alvinellid* worms
lapping up the heat of the vent kitchen.

Now the ground was opening up
under her feet
and there was nothing but worms.

Cancer worms multiplying through Daniel.
Huge heartache worms colonising her.

Extremophiles all.

They loved the heat. They adored
the cold.

She was disappearing.
Daniel was dying.
The worms were thriving.

Shellgrit

Pedicabo ego vos et irrumabo
Aureli pathice et cinaede Furi
Daniel scrapes Catullus's rape threat
out from under his nails
  and makes the threat his own

I will rape the both of you
  as each of you deserves
you in the arse, Phoebe,
  you in the mouth, Alex

would future slow-blooded critics
  say of him
    as they said of Catullus
that he doesn't mean it
  a poem can only play?

oh little would they know
of poetry
oh little would they know
of him

The worm farm

It takes all Daniel's
courage
to open the lid
of the worm farm

but it would take even more
courage
to ask Alex.

The worm farm
is his job.

He would prefer a box
of red-eyed rats
to this seething face
of his own fate.

He reaches for the familiarly useless
comfort
of common sense

they're just worms
they're good for the garden

but reaching into the writhing dirt
is like putting his arm
down the mouth of a tiger shark
and feeling each row of teeth
grow.

THE STARS

The apricot tree

Daniel fights
the chemo nausea
smoking a joint
in the late five o'clock sun

he's getting better
at cutting Alex out
hunched over her computer
in a dark humid room

he slows his breathing
comfortably
as the good dope
kicks in
and notices the pearly half-moon
in the faded blue sky
hanging over the apricot tree.

With a quick delight
he sees the rough old tree
is starting to blossom
struggling a bit

with frail bits of stick
waving heavy white blossoms

Daniel rubs
his own heart hard

come on   he prays
come on

The rainbow

We both shut our eyes
the last terrible time
we tried sex.

I felt his hurt,
perhaps hatred,
when I came on his fingers
not his struggling dick.

Were we *both* thinking
of Phoebe?

But over champagne
this lovely twilight,
with the roses
still drenched and scenting
heavy
from the late afternoon
storm,
we're open-eyed
as if all our drinks together
still count.

It's Daniel
who first sees the rainbow,
arching in the aery blue
beyond our garden.

'Look' he says
and takes my hand
loosely,
until the rainbow
fades out
with the squabbling cries
of the roosting lorikeets.

Seduction

It was the light
ravishing Daniel
like a seduction
he'd never known
like a fever
that had never ravaged him.

It was the light
tawny and strange
raging through the flickering
leaves of the apricot tree.

The light
the twilight light
coming for him
like a slow swelling sea
coming for him
a rippling salty eternity.

Beautiful little buggers

'Check out
these beautiful little buggers'
Rachel holds up to the light
grainy photos—

moons and worms,
slugs, balloons
and squiggles
of teeming bacteria.

I take them
wordlessly in

'Guess where I got them . . .'

'Where?' my nose
floods with cold, spicy air

'Santa Claus has moved
to the South Pole, sweetheart'

'Lake Vostok?'

Rachel nods
grinning

'In an ice core'
I gnaw my cheek
'or from the water?'

Rachel leans forward

'We did it. Pay dirt.
From the water.'

'Contamination?
Rachel, remember the Mars meteorite.
Are you sure . . .?'

Or is it me
smelling hot metal
hearing a dirty hum
as the secret
subterranean pristine lake
trembles?

Rachel,
    completely out of character,
kisses my hand

'Say it,' she whispers
'say it after me—

Europa   Europa
here we come!'

Selfish

My life is fucked.

Sweet merciless Time
be my deliverance.

Take my dying husband.
Take my absent lacerating lover.

Bring me the morning
when I'm heartened back
to my selfish self again.

The hard bright morning
that will bang my elbow
back to smarting
good work.

Purgatory

I'm getting too comfortable
picnicking with Dante
in the Inferno

like a porpoising sinner
flashing his arse
in the boiling pitch
I'm getting the hang
of the place

it's time
for the character-building
vicissitudes of Purgatory

where you are purified
by flame
and intense boredom

but unlike Hell
and just like marriage
it doesn't last forever.

Famous

He wakes up early
tasting brass in his mouth.

Is it a stale stray trumpet
from his wife's brass band?

She's on the radio.
She's on TV.

Does she never weary
of her yakkety yak celebrity?

Daniel slithers green-eyed
  and monstrous
    along the Purgatorial terraces
and gloats over Alex
   suffering the hard slog
     of pride's punishment.

Crushed under her penitential
     stone
her nose rubbed in her own dirt

    and ashes
she wouldn't see the stars
    let alone be one.

Daniel takes a gulp
  of warmish bedside water,
he's starting to really
  hate her

and there's no penance
  for hatred

only a hell, a foul taste,
  of self.

Alex wakes up
  quickly as always
then leaning on her long
  brown arm
smiles deliciously
  into his eyes

and his heart turns
  over

with my nasty mind
with my failing body
   I Thee Worship.

Beatrice

Will she be waiting for me
on the other side
of the bite of fire?

Unlike Dante
I'm easy about flames.

I have no memory
of the church's dogged mercy
bar as a kid
when a few fervent born-agains
had a bash at my soul.

I have no memory
of scorching stakes
and the pious stink
of blackening flesh.

Instead I've shared
with Dante
the fanatical faith of Poetry,
and the faith in Love

with gleaming
even amused eyes
waiting on the other side
of my life shivering through
the wall of fire.

Will Love lovingly
take me to task too?
I would so relish
receiving the rough side
of her tongue.

I'll know, like Dante,
my exile is over.

Love

During my good moments
I want to hold Alex in my arms
and tell her everything will be
all right.

It's not that fabled peace
of the dying.
I don't feel a bit peaceful.
Nor generosity of spirit.
I've forgiven nothing.

It's love.

Love still scuttling about
in my heart
like a greedy crab, claws akimbo.

Love that's hanging on.

Love that doesn't hoard
its staling miseries and betrayals.
Love that walks out at dawn,

like an exhausted Pushkin
with pistol, pride and poetry
to fight for his beautiful stupid wife's honour.

Love, like Pushkin,
that gets shot horribly in the guts
and still takes forever to die.

Penance

Every morning
Alex embraced the ritual
of Daniel's coffee.

With fanatical gratitude
she carried its Cross
walked its Stations
taking her pilgrim's time
to make it divinely
perfect.

She carried it on a tray
garnished with chocolate biscuits
he was always too sick
to eat.

She'd perch on the end
of their bed
chattering to him
while he took his first
shaky sips.

'Is it OK, darling?'

she'd ask
as if wanting him
one morning
to show her some real mercy

and make her do it
all over again.

Struggle

The world's too precious—
my soul's knuckles
bone-white
from hanging on—

the sun on my chest.
the crimson toothbrush
first flowers on the grevillea
Alex and I chose together
never thinking—

what?

it's Spring
beautiful. jasmine scented.
floating around me
like—

what?

not a one-night stand chemise.
not one of her remote gorgeous
nursery nebulas—

what?

is it the purplish new leaves
on the lemon tree?

remembering it was
    our lemon tree
    our lemon tree

The Peace Rose

This morning I know
where my blessings lie—
in my garden.

Now I don't have to wait
for the yard-arm
I drink when I like—
and enjoy my smokes too.

Why is the flute of champagne
in my hand quivering?

I have stopped crying
over myself
and my life's unweeded waste.

Why is my hand quivering
while there is the just-opened
peace rose
opulently fragrant to steady me?

My eyes flood
with its succulent colour
like the pulp of a sweet peach.

Let me water the rose's roots
with my jittery gratitude
   and a good splash of champagne.

On the stroke

It's just a stroke away
from midnight
on New Year's Eve
I insisted Alex go out
and leave me
in bed with Dante

and unlike the living poet
guided down the stinking
circles of Hell
tonight I don't think
I'm casting a shadow

have I died already?

Would I feel more
substantial
if I were in Hell?

Because tonight
I am not feeling
anything.

The clean soft sheets
the exquisite company
of great poetry
a glass of going-warm
champagne
the warm black
summer night air

there is a peaceful fragrance
somewhere

the new year waiting
fresh and untainted
just outside the window

and now
the shrieks   an illegal bang
acrid smell of firecrackers

pop
arrives the new year
like a big relieved gulp.

I stroke a page of Dante
and wish it were his
palpable living poet's
face

because tonight
I'm not feeling anything.

My midnight house

I'm waiting for my midnight snake
  in my midnight house

I'm waiting with an Etruscan smile
  and a leper's rattle

I'm waiting like Cleopatra
  quippy and finished

O asp! O black beautiful bite!

In my midnight house
  morphine stays up with me
    as we happily watch
      my life's fanged movies
        fizzling away.

Red giant

Was Daniel really dying
  or was he instead
slowly unconsciously
slowly deliberately
  shrivelling her?

Don't the dying shrink
  and cool,
rather than growing bigger
  and hotter
like a red giant sun
  dying in a horrifying bloat
    across its planets?

She couldn't pity him anymore,
he was a cosmic catastrophe
he was boiling away
all her seas.

Ride a Macbeth

This morning I'm leaking
rotten egg gas
and I can't bear Dante.

Because everything
even in the muck
of Hell
sounds too deliciously fun
in Italian.

Let me ride on a black blast
of hammer-hard English.

Tomorrow, and tomorrow, and tomorrow

Let me ride Macbeth's beat
like a broomstick
while I screech along
to his idiot's foul tale.

Pain is murdering me.

But leaving me with the bit
and bite
of my own tongue's
bolting and unforgiving
poetry.

Help! Another Day!

Can I scream to you, Emily?
  All in spinsterish white
  straight as a finger
  at the end of my bed.

Blazing white—
  oh Emily
  your poems were never
  so bloody obvious.

White-out.
  Emily, I'm abusing you
    like a morphine drip

my veins are hugging you
  with a purely selfish
    squeezing need

the letting go

Emily, is that my wife
 in tears again?

The Martian Meteorite

Alex needed the drink.

Her fingers gratefully chill
on the clammy surface
of the pub glass.

The wine tastes sour
burning through her chest
but she gulps it down
like a beer.

And Daniel
 unshaved, sweating and twitching
 in his morphine doze
begins to dim
in her aching head.

Rachel is drunk and gabbling,
but her yak has a confessional
claw
and yanks Alex in.

'Alex, I've always been
a gutless wonder.

I sat shtum
when they threw out
the meteorite.

I was shit-scared.
I can't tell you
how many reputations
have smashed
on that fucking rock.

But I know bugs
when I see them.

You know me.
I live and dream
bacteria.

Christ knows about Europa.
But I'm telling you, Alex,
Mars is alive.'

The life zone

Driving home in the exhausting
becalmed
of the last few weeks
Alex's mind crawls
into Rachel's meteorite,
looking among
the trapped Martian gases
and controversial
microscopic scribbles
not so much for signatures
of extinct alien life
but for living refuge and comfort.

There was nothing more
to be done for Daniel.

It was impossible to know
if he was at peace with her
or himself.

He was now in his dying
even more mysterious
than the Martian meteorite.

And when he finally moved out
of the life zone
what frustrating silent fossils
would he permanently embed
in Alex's heart?

Dante's stars

Outside the sky darkens
and a silent wind is rippling
through the silver leaves
of a massive old gum tree

some sleepy last sense
drifting through Daniel,
like a last guest finding his own way
out,
wonders at the warm something
clutching his relaxed hand

but he's mostly
fully occupied.

This is the highest climb
he has ever done.

Who would have thought
he would feel so light

or is it still Virgil
doing all the work?

He must make it up to him
later
when they get to the top.

For now
there's this bottleneck
this last squeeze

Alex, his hand
breathes its last

suddenly he knows
just before knowing and seeing
fuse

he's climbed up
by climbing down

and once more saw
the stars

The company of breathing men

What of Daniel
now he has left
  the company of breathing men?

He's tossing
  quite pleasantly
on a water whirl of memory
  like a jellyfish enjoying
    a boisterous high tide

and he remembers distantly
    promising Alex
that he would lovingly
    haunt her
      if he ever died first.

But he doesn't
    and he won't.

He is being tossed
  and taken
somewhere beyond

   the gritty shores
      of married love

then something stings through him
    with an unearthly thrill

every angel is terrifying

beyond the tug
 of a hoarse grief
    dawdling fainter and fainter
     behind him
he is changing
   into a hungry fish
rapidly gilled
   to dart and glitter
     towards the exciting ether
       beyond the stars.

Nudo come un verme

They brought Giordano Bruno
to the Campo de' Fiori
nudo come un verme

tongue spiked
he couldn't ensnare
the roaring Roman crowd
with a last whirling word
of heresy

tongue spiked
he could still
dismiss the cross
and look ostentatiously
skywards
straight into the morning sun

in a blaze of orange flame
and flesh-pungent smoke
his dying
is crackling eloquently
in Alex's shivering sleep

as she lies sprawled
on her belly
nudo come un verme

she wakes up
biting her tongue
in a sweat of pain
and panic

Bruno she mumbles
thickly to the dark
help me   help me

Daniel's legacy

Why was Daniel's mother
lingering
in the post-wake mess
of half-empty bottles
and half-bitten crudités?

Was it that famed bloody
Irish blood
that can't leave a party?

Gulping down
a huge impatient fatigue
Alex approaches her
with as tender a daughter-in-law
smile
as she can dredge.

'Sheila' she says softly
touching the older woman
awkwardly
on her fat mottled arm.

'What was he all about?'
Daniel's mother mutters
'Just *what* was he all about?'

And Alex slumps
under the memory
of all the phone calls,
all the drives
to the outer suburbs,
all the loving tedium
of family outgrown,
Daniel had so cunningly
dodged.

'I'll show you'
she finally answers
guiding Daniel's mother
into his musty study.

'This'
Alex points
at Daniel's high-rise blocks
of lonely poetry

tottering over them
'this
is what he was about.'

Daniel's mother nods
her untidy grey head

then quietly curses
'I know
'cause he bloody well
got it from me.'

Antarctic heartbreak

Two weeks after Daniel died
Rachel rings,
her raucous anguish
wrapping around Alex's face
like ether

'We've killed Lake Vostok!'

Rachel's repulsive sobbing
is making Alex gag

and she doesn't want to hear
any more,
doesn't want to feel the cracking
death
of the nurturing ice,
doesn't want to see the oily murk
of the violated water.

'Thirty million years' worth
of new bugs.

all gone.'
Rachel howls down the phone

'We're not scientists any more, Alex,
we're thieves
the kind that smash down your door
and leave their shit on your walls.

Rape
is too sweet a word
for what that hydrobot did.

It burnt and shat its way
through the ice,
and the only images
it showed us
were of its self
dying in a convulsion
of leaking fuel

killing the lake with it'

Under ice

Is this how Lake Vostok
used to feel?

Like me?
Suspended in frigid blackness.

It's not so flash
living under ice.

Maybe we did her
a favour.

Change is always
a bit mucky.

Maybe Lake Vostok was longing
for our hot drill.

Longing for the excitement
of contamination.

Maybe that's how life
moves forward.

Something dies.
Something much
more remarkable

comes into grubby bloody
being.

Extinction

Waking up in icy sheets
Alex feels an arctic tentacle
suck hard and cruel
on her aching leg

where was Marlowe?

was he still curled up grieving
in Daniel's old black
jumper?

where.   where was Daniel?

and the long cold tongue
of extinction
licks Alex's ear

he's with me   in the Martian sea

THE GARDEN

Honeyeaters (2)

The sky is darkening.
The computer screen glows
heartlessly
in the dim of Alex's study.

She looks out the window.
The garden is parched,
the grevillea waves thirstily
at her.

She keeps forgetting to water.

rain for christ's sake rain

but she's living through a taunting
drought
where the sky keeps darkening
without relenting into rain.

She leaves her work,
which is reeking
of stale nagging failure,

and wanders with Marlowe
out to the apricot tree,
longing for a spitting
on her face
and a rumbling give in the air

instead she hears the return
of the darting tiny honeyeaters
come out chittering
to relish
the chilly dry stillness.

Thunderstorm on Jupiter

It's drizzling outside.
Yesterday's heat wave
gone.

Alex watches the rain collecting
like a fur of dew
on the thinly tapering leaves
of Daniel's grevillea,
then notices
some of its leaves
are raggedly munched.

What would Daniel do?

She nibbles
at her useless numbness
and turning her back to the window
conjures herself
flying through a thunderhead
on violently alive Jupiter.

How big a lightning bolt
would it take
to crack her ice?

Crack her wide open
to the risk and thrill
of living again.

Questions from the floor

Insomnia loves meetings.

Insomnia likes them best
with endless belligerent questions
from the floor.

Daniel, why can't we laugh off
these deranged ratbags
like we always did?

Even Europa has joined the mob,
too proud and distant
to use the mike,
asks me whispering
*what do you really know
about me?*

Daniel, don't leave me
it gets worse.

Lake Vostok slops to its feet
and doesn't have to ask anything

but hold up grime-slicked
empty hands
and point the finger

Your parrots

Can the colour of grass
overwhelm you like music?

Hold you taut and tearful
like a violin stringing you
up?

But something's moving in it
like a nest of rats.

A flock of parrots.

Oh Daniel   red-rumped parrots!

Bugger them.
They're in sticky pairs.

Don't hold the domesticity
of parrots
against me
now you're dead.

But please
keep thumping in my head
rip through my brain blood barrier
if you must

infect me   give me
your songs.   your parrots.

You once asked me

Daniel, you once asked me—
    belligerently—
if I'd loved Phoebe
 as much as I'd loved you
  'at the beginning'

beginning
  oh christ, darling,
I remember how your voice
    broke
on the wheel
  of that word.

Daniel, my Daniel,
  can I talk honestly
   to you now?

Your ghost
  a far better listener
than you ever were—

though I do miss
  your snorting acerbic
interruptions.

I never loved Phoebe
as I loved you.

Not at the beginning.

Not at
the end.

Like Europa she was a mystery
I wanted to conquer
and crack.

And like Europa
she had the last numbing
word.

But you, darling,
were no ice-crusted
speck
teasing me
from a cold night sky.

You were always
ardently present.

You loved me more
than I ever loved Phoebe
or Europa.

You were the champagne
glass
desperate to be heard—

right there singing
in my careless hand.

The only lemon

Daniel had adored the lemon
tree,
clucking over its one and only
lemon

'it's getting bigger'

he would say

'look, I can see
a bit of yellow,
give it a week
and we'll celebrate its ripening
in a gin and tonic'

they never did

Daniel died,
and the lemon
was still green,
and growing
infinitesimally slowly

some late afternoons
Alex would wander out
with Marlowe
on a lemon walk

she suspected
that the lemon
would still be there
green and growing
after she herself
had died

the lemon had a kind
of perverse defiance,
refusing to grow up,
refusing to be plucked
sliced and floated
in someone's moment
of sweet alcoholic
clink and epiphany

it was an infuriating lemon,
but it seemed to hold
some secret

to time dilation,
and Alex, on strange silent
afternoons
after Daniel's death,
almost believed
that the lemon
was slowing her own life down,
her own fatal ripening.

Early morning terrestrial

Admit it.
There's no birdsong on Europa.

When the tiny sun rises
over the blinding bergs and cliffs
there is a silence
so loud
it would stone your heart.

This morning,
behind the lace-work
of foggy gum trees,
a currawong is calling
Alex awake
calling
like a sun-pinging creek.

Giant squid

I dreamt last night
that I lay naked
at the bottom
of a soft black sea
in the many loving arms
of a giant squid

our strange
mutually enraptured
breathing
in perfect unison
as we nibbled on
each other's preciously
alien faces.

At the back of my purring mind
was an itch for a camera,
to show the world
my lover, my monster mollusc,
truly existed.

But in my dream
I didn't move.

There was a terrific tranquillity
in just lying still
and not proving anything.

Daniel's Poetry Reading List

The Complete Poems of Anna Akhmatova—translated by Judith Hemschemeyer (Canongate Press, Edinburgh, 1992)

Selected Poems—W.H. Auden (Faber, London, 1938)

The Complete Works of William Blake (Thomas and Hudson, London, 1978)

The Poems of Catullus (Penguin Classics, Great Britain, 1966)

Catullus—Charles Martin (Hermes Books, Yale, 1992)

The Complete Poems of Cavafy—translated by Rae Dalven (Harcourt USA, Orlando, 1976)

Coleridge—Selected Poems (Oxford University Press, Oxford, 1965)

The Divine Comedy. 2 Purgatory—Dante Alighieri—translated by Dorothy L. Sayers (Penguin Classics, Great Britain, 1974)

The Inferno of Dante—translated by Robert Pinsky (Farrar, Straus and Giroux, New York, 1994)

Purgatorio—Dante Alighieri—translated by W.S. Merwin (Knopf, New York, 2000)

Emily Dickinson—The Complete Poems (Faber, London, 1970)

Selections of Keats (Methuen, London, 1934)

Philip Larkin—Collected Poems (Faber, London, 1988)

Li Po and Tu Fu (Penguin Classics, Great Britain, 1973)

The Complete Plays—Christopher Marlowe (The Penguin English Library, London, 1986)

The Poems of Andrew Marvell (The Muses Library, London, 1952)

The Metamorphoses of Ovid—translated by David R. Slavitt (John Hopkins University Press, Baltimore and London, 1994)

Sylvia Plath—Collected Poems (Faber, London, 1981)

Eugene Onegin—Alexander Pushkin—translated by Charles Johnston (Penguin Classics, London, 1977)

The Selected Poetry of Rainer Maria Rilke—edited and translated by Stephen Mitchell (Pan Books, London, 1987)

Sappho—translated by Mary Barnard (Shambhala Pocket Classics, Boston, 1994)

William Shakespeare—*Macbeth* (Penguin, Harmondsworth, 1967)

Sophocles—*The Theban Plays* (Penguin, Harmondsworth, 1947)

W.B. Yeats—Selected Poetry (Macmillan, London, 1965)

Notes

67	Title from 'The Kraken' by Alfred Lord Tennyson
85–86	Title and quotes from 'On First Looking Into Chapman's Homer' by John Keats
90	Title and quotes from 'The Garden' by Andrew Marvell
123	Title and quotes from *The War of the Worlds* by H.G. Wells
185	Title from 'In Memory of W.B. Yeats' by W.H. Auden
208	Title and quotes from 'Archaic Torso of Apollo' by Rainer Maria Rilke
247	Title from 'Midnight verses' by Anna Akhmatova
251	Title and quotes from poetry of Emily Dickinson
257	Quote from closing lines of 'The Inferno' by Dante Alighieri
258	Title and quote from 'Purgatory' by Dante Alighieri.
259	Quote from 'Duino Elegies' by Rainer Maria Rilke

Dorothy Porter
What a Piece of Work

'I've scratched your soul'
  Frank whispers
    fighting the needle
      with clenched tooth
        and clenched claw

'Count to ten, Frank'
  I say gently

'I've scratched ...'

Frank's eyes flickering
  but still fighting

as he goes under.

As the new Superintendent at Callan Park Psychiatric Hospital, Dr Peter Cyren must perform medical alchemy—turn diseased minds into healthy ones. But in the case of his own soul, this sacred process works irrevocably in reverse.

Crackling with style, Dorothy Porter's stunning *What a Piece of Work* is a poetic masterpiece.

Dorothy Porter
The Monkey's Mask

The Monkey's Mask is a totally unique experience. It's poetry. It's a crime thriller. It's where high art meets low life, passion meets betrayal, and poetry faces profanity on the streets of a harsh modern city. Dorothy Porter's internationally bestselling verse novel holds you in its grip from the first verse paragraph to the final haunting pages.

What the critics said about *The Monkey's Mask:*

'a beautiful, slippery, wholly felt epic of love, betrayal and murder that you have to restrain yourself from reading at one sitting'
THE INDEPENDENT

'a tour de force that manages to be a complex thriller, a state-of-the-gender sexual novel and a convincingly lyrical on-rush of poetry'
Peter Porter, THE AGE

Has a twist you won't soon forget. Put off by the idea of crime in verse? Don't be'
KIRKUS REVIEWS

'It strips the noir thriller down to its bare essentials, leaving its dense, moral, erotic, gut-churning ambience intact and clutching the reader with a grip like a talon round the throat'
Val McDermid, MANCHESTER EVENING STANDARD

'Dorothy Porter has combined two barely-related genres, and created an unusual heroine, and she has done so with breathtaking innovation. Her poems are short, powerful, beautiful and sometimes brutal. Each poem is a portrait, a sensation, a short story, a joke, or a reflection in itself'
THE TIMES

'very funny. Caustic humour. Porter makes her narrator able to fix a character in just a few words'
TIMES LITERARY SUPPLEMENT

WINNER OF THE AGE POETRY BOOK OF THE YEAR 1994

Dorothy Porter
Other Worlds—Poems 1997–2001

But what difference
  does the looking
  of a finite terrestrial
  neurally-aglow mammal
  really make?

Deep space. Jupiter. Medellin. Olympic Sydney. Europa. Northern Territory. Other worlds …

Where *The Monkey's Mask* showed poetry could be 'sticky as sex', *Other Worlds* burns poetry in after-images on the retina, illuminating the strangeness, grit and beauty of life at the beginning of the twenty-first century. This is high velocity poetry questioning contemporary living with savage wit.